ADAPTED BY **Teresa Mlawer**   ILLUSTRATED BY **Olga Cuéllar**

The Tortoise and the Hare

Adirondack
Books

Once upon a time there was a hare who boasted that he could run faster than anyone.

He was always teasing the tortoise because she was too slow.

One sunny summer day, the tortoise was walking slowly along the forest enjoying the beautiful scenery.

Suddenly, the hare crossed her path, and making fun of her said, "What's the big rush?"

Upset by his comment, the tortoise said,

"Why do you make fun of me? No one doubts you are a fast runner, but the faster runner is not always the one who wins the race."

Upon hearing this, the hare started laughing.

"Who is going to beat me? You? That's really silly! There is no one who can beat me. I am the fastest runner in the world! I challenge you to a race."

The tortoise, annoyed at the hare's bragging, accepted the challenge.

Plans for the race were soon underway, and the race was set to take place at dawn the very next day.

The morning of the race, all the forest animals gathered at the starting line.

Everyone thought that the hare would win, but secretly, they were rooting for the tortoise.

At the agreed time, the duck, with a loud QUACK-QUACK, gave the signal to start the race.

The hare began leaping and running very fast, while the tortoise plodded along.

The hare was confident he was way ahead of
the slow moving tortoise. But since he was still a little
tired from getting up so early for the race, he decided
it would be a good time to take a rest.

He turned back to the tortoise and teasingly said, "Take your time. I'm going to rest for a while and if you pass me, I'll catch up with you in a minute."

When the hare woke up, he realized that he still had a good lead over the tortoise, who had barely covered a short distance.

Since the hare did not have breakfast that morning,
he decided to stop and munch on some lettuce sprouts
he saw growing on the side of the road.

The hare felt sleepy after having too much to eat under the hot sun. After checking that he still had a lead over the tortoise, he decided to take a nap under the shadow of an oak tree.

In the meantime, the tortoise continued to advance slowly but surely. Tired but determined, she lifted her long neck and was happy to see that she was very close to the finish line.

It was precisely at that moment, upon hearing the cheers from the crowd, that the hare woke up with a startle.

When he realized that the tortoise was very
close to the finish line, he got up with a jolt
and started jumping and running.

Everyone was screaming, dancing, and clapping for the tortoise.

Realizing that the hare was very close behind, the tortoise gave one last push, stretched her long neck as far as she could, and touched the finish line first. The tortoise had won the race!

The hare, exhausted, collapsed beside the happy tortoise. Even though the hare didn't win, he learned a good lesson: the faster runner is not always the one who wins the race.

What lesson have we learned from this fable?

If you persevere and try your best you can succeed.

TEXT COPYRIGHT ©2016 BY TERESA MLAWER / ILLUSTRATIONS COPYRIGHT©2016 BY ADIRONDACK BOOKS

FOR INFORMATION, PLEASE CONTACT ADIRONDACK BOOKS, P.O. BOX 266, CANANDAIGUA, NEW YORK, 14424

ISBN 978-0-9864313-4-0   10 9 8 7 6 5 4 3 2 1   PRINTED IN CHINA